# Entropocene

# Other Titles from
# Space Cowboy Books

## Books:

One Way & Other Stories – Miriam Allen deFord

Space Exploration: Strange New Worlds – John C. Mannone

Life During the Lazarus Age – Robert Frazier

Dreaming of Autonomous Vehicles – Jaroslav Olša, Jr.

The Future is Brief – Jean-Paul L. Garnier

Wave IX – Various Authors

The Martians – Emilie Procházková

Mexicans on the Moon – Pedro Iniguez

Another Time: Time Travel Stories 1942–1960

Complete Poems 1965–2020 – Michael Butterworth

Simultaneous Times Vol. 3 – Various Authors

Simultaneous Times Vol. 2.5 – Various Authors

Simultaneous Times Vol. 2 – Various Authors

Simultaneous Times Vol. 1 – Various Authors

Garbage In, Gospel Out – Jean-Paul L. Garnier

Betelgeuse Dimming – Jean-Paul L. Garnier

Future Anthropology – Jean-Paul L. Garnier

## Chapbooks:

The Reducing Flame – Richard Magahiz

Micropoetry for Microplanets – Brian U. Garrison

Shelf Life – F. J. Bergmann

Mars Maundering – Denise Dumars

**www.spacecowboybooks.com**

# Entropocene

Jean-Paul L. Garnier

ISBN: 978-1-968958-02-2

First Edition | 2025

Space Cowboy Books

61871 29 Palms Hwy.
Joshua Tree, CA 92252
www.spacecowboybooks.com

# Table of Contents

# Introduction

I often write in thematic clusters. Many of the poems in this collection started off as themed chapbooks, where I took the opportunity to explore a concept with a set of poems, each looking at my topic from a different angle. Speculative poetry sometimes serves me as a proving ground to explore concepts that I may want to write fiction about, allowing me to test out my ideas to see how far they can be stretched, if they will fall flat, or if they can blossom from a few lines into something larger and possibly book length. The three chapbooks collected here took on the themes of Utopia, Time, and Telepathy: all cornerstones of the science fiction genre. I wanted to address the complicated problems that arise from each of these concepts, and to take them on in brief bursts of energy. Because of this method, some of the poems may not land on their own but together build up a more coherent picture of my thoughts on the matter, which is exactly why they originally appeared as small, self-contained chapbooks. Writing with one specific theme in mind can be challenging, and sometimes a theme is exhausted before it can grow into a collection, yet I still find this method to be a good way of exploring my ideas. The miscellaneous poems in this collection were mostly written as standalone works and published in various speculative fiction magazines and anthologies.

After working for years as a poetry editor, I have found that I write less poetry and have turned to longer forms to tell my stories. But poetry will always be my first love when it comes to writing, and although I write less of it these days it will always be a part of my writing life. The brevity and concise manner in which poetry can convey thoughts and feelings will always strike me as a pure form of storytelling, and I have attempted to bring its lessons into the way that I write fiction.

Still, you'll often find me scribbling away on poems, seeing where the ideas can take me, and which form my narratives are wanting to take. As an aphant my poems tend not to be image based, but rather designed to draw out rich emotional responses to the bewilderment of being alive. Some have called my poems "punchy," and this always pleases me, as at times I will use the rhythms of boxing to inform the structure of the poetry. Rhythm is one of poetry's possible strong points and I hope that you find the rhythms employed enjoyable, even if at times they may be jarring.

Jean-Paul L. Garnier
Joshua Tree, CA
October 2025

UTOPIAN
PROBLEMS

## Small Utopias

always an island
cut off somehow
perhaps it is the greater scale
that complicates our anarchy
or wealth must always produce the poor
at whose expense Le Guin's nightmare
are there too many
of us for peace
for bounty, plentitude, enough for each
or surplus has forever killed
along with ownership, free-will
or to live in love means servitude
though egos crush this attitude
wanting for more
disturbs the balance
would you choose greed
or meet the challenge

**Possibility**

if Utopia is impossible
then how have we dreamt
for so long
whose lie are we following
whose tipped scale
bountiful Earth
trampled under the feet
    of profit
this is not the stewardship
    we dreamt
but we dream
    full of possibility
we dream

**Equalizing Our Worth, Accepting Flaws**

I can carry your weight
for a time
who, today, will be the strong one
we must take turns
accept our flaws
know what to do
when we are both weak
when we are both strong

this cannot be done at some's expense
hold each other up with confidence

that we are not the same
must be the Cause
and I'll carry your weight
despite our flaws

**Global Contact, Neighborly Love**

a kind word
given freely
passed from one hand to another
and taking its time
traveling far and long
reaches all the way across the world

an ill glance
does the same

the echo will resound
nothing to stop the contagious
as it gains momentum
taking its time
passes through us all
how many times
until the glance
becomes the word
changing the world
forever

**Can We Agree**

a sine wave looking for the zero point
three per cycle
dialectic beats away
one would think consistency would cause agreement

we give our hopes the name of No Place
pessimistic optimism
defeated at conception
all want a better future, fewer truly believe

why should ideal be too grand
          if we've dreamt for a thousand years
or power wielded in wrong hands
difficult to forgive
in high demand, learn not their lesson, rise above

we must agree, collaborate, design for commonality
we've labored for war
the very last time
the goals are clear
now shake hands, decide

**Skills / One of Each**

like bees, like ants
roles are flexible
overcrowded similarities
tip and sink the ship

now is the time
for strengths to come forward
you there, plumber – hold my hand
vitality in each

dream into function
leaves less time for dreaming
for here
the dream must manifest

## Art Won't Be Enough

give my pen to the architect
hand me a shovel
my meat may be more useful
than my mind

give my knife to the hunter
may there be nothing to defend

give my repose to the wind
there is work to do

give my ideas to the collective
let the group decide

give my youth to the young
all elders to parent

give my poems to the fire
let us warm by these energies together

**Reconciling Faith**

if we achieve balance
can this be our belief
the unmoving force
which binds in harmony

can this be our strength
if our values differ
may every rivulet
combine to form our river

which we share
to slake our thirst
our movements into energy
differences wound into a chord
which strengthens us collectively

## How Shall We Teach Our Young

hierarch of trades
will not work
lest we stagnate

let them choose
fragile balances
interfere

two roles each
alternating shifts
labors require
less than we want

as a machine we must move
versatile parts
demanding no less than perfection, individuality
for the grand
sacrifice must be common

## Will They Kill Us

in grand tradition
as we move into a better world
separate in our attempt to unite
grander purpose
will they kill us for doing so
will success threaten
the status quo we try to fix
autonomy has no place
in the world system of wealth
so they kill those
practicing new models

do we defend ourselves
becoming all
which we try to leave behind
small groups may trade
trade blows or goods
it does not appear the same
from all angles

**Am I Useful**

in a perfect society
one would know their place
knowing one's place
could be demeaning, or not
are we told or do we choose
are my skills of any use

**Resources**

with nothing
    nothing to fight over
with nothing
    we share
how much nothing
    would it take
        to build our freedom

accumulation is the risk
    if you can't carry it
    leave it behind
for the next guy
    may be in need

nothing's coming with us anyway

# Time's Arrow

if the cup breaks
then I drop it
effect becomes cause
if this / then
both directions point
toward chaos
this 2D view
ignores the expanding sphere
direction becomes infinite points
Planck length and perfect
the arrow freezes
when velocity and position
cannot meet
observer collects
ordering shards into cups
the mess goes away
and entropy is a state of mind

when time is over
now will be the last
present you receive

you ask for seconds
currently
you'd better work on your timing
forever isn't happening

slipping past eternity

**Time's Extended Warranty**

while exceptions have been made in the past
heat death voids this warranty
don't hesitate
no better time than the present
when any instant
brief as it may be
could wind down like a broken clock
this sale will pass in the blink of an eye
so, act now without pause

time machine broken
electronics era
predates industrial

∞

past self
passes by
young forever

time's arrow
knows not straight lines
released, it arced
rose from the chaos
to order – ever so briefly
then gently fell
hitting entropy's mark
as all stood still
     in that last eternal moment

time's up
when the clock strikes
you fail to punch in
now
all the time in the world
is only one moment
until you ride the cycle
past the future and present
back to the delicious past
twice upon that time
upon that time
you come upon a time
when time is not up

when the clock strikes
you fail to punch in

**The Zone**

as the athlete, the musician
slows time
as panic and fear
stretch time
as joy and sex
speed time
as growth and age
draw out and compress time
as labor and the mundane
drag time
as watching the clock
freezes time
emanating from glands
time is a function
of hormone

in the beginning
it was the present
in the end
it will be the present
when time slips
instantly infinitude obliterates time
and it will still be the present

folded like an accordion
Damascus steel
croissant
the only straight lines
in nature, belong to the mind
biological construct
in a cosmos of spirals
counting our circumnavigations
never actually returning
corkscrewing into the wine-like void

emerge, take flight larvae
eat – mate – die
time flies
never to see a sunset
a day, your forever

brevity, whose eyes measure you
perhaps the compound
variety of perspective
perceives the passage relatively

and human,
your time flies
despite abstracting, counting
in your Planck moment
time still flies

→
Abruptly
Beginning　　　Eon
New　　　　　　　　Ends
↑ Presents　　　∞　　　　　Now ↓
Simultaneously　　Pending
Time　　Interim
When
←

infinity
all that carrier light
may diffuse
reduce me to lone photon
the timeless particle
waves goodbye
forever

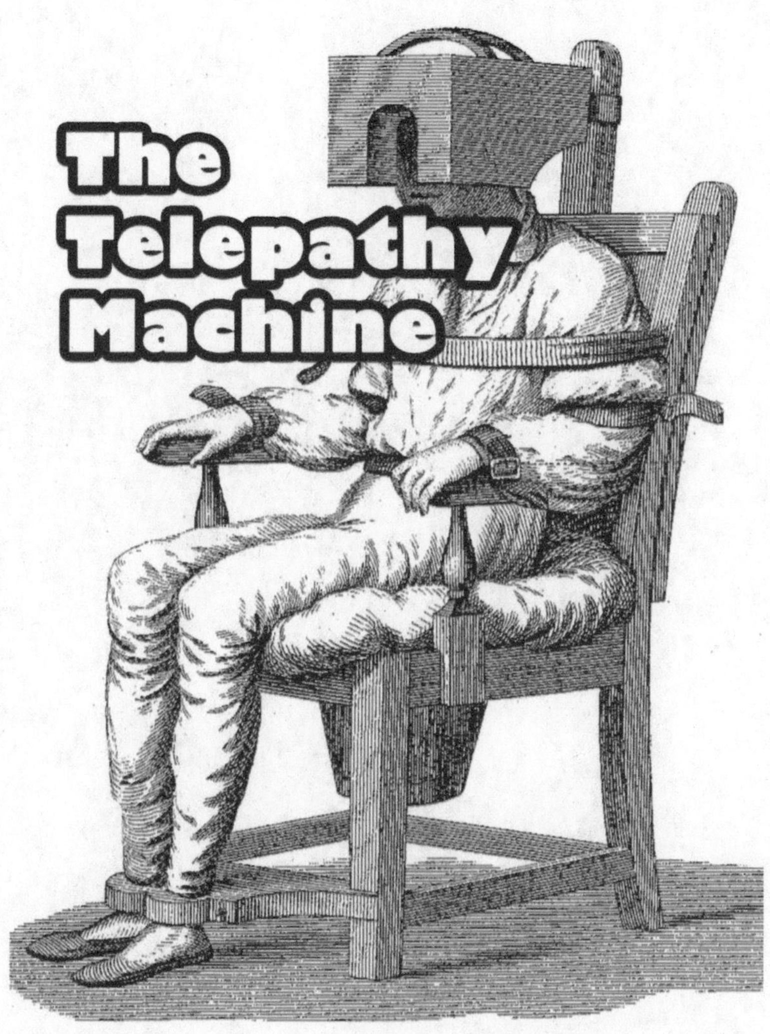
The
Telepathy
Machine

**The Wish**

I wish I could read your mind
we could be as one
    stripped of individuality
    never alone
we'd have no secrets
    no privacy
finish each other's sentences
    always interrupting
completely transparent
    unfiltered raw nerve
fully understand each other
    misread in moments of clarity
I wish I could read your mind
    but would you understand

**The Telepathy Machine**

the telepathy machine worked perfectly
too much so
two layers of thought
our goal achieved, was overwhelming
still, doable
our layered minds seldom speak to singular subjects
the thoughts were not shocking
'whoa' was the consensus
however, the sensations
confused bouquets of scent, poorly mixing
tactile floods of skin
3D landscapes jumbled, superimposed
confounded bodily pain
variations of color
every sound echoing
visual triangulation, too many eyes
if no observer had milled near
neither of us could have located the off switch

**Signal to Noise**

we learned to tune
down to only us two
thinking to avoid the cacophony
thinking
the problem remained
together
at once
interrupting
the gaps between words
filled with mortar-like noise

**Honesty**

they thought they were honest
we heard those thoughts too
we all did
misconception, even of oneself
clattered back all percussive
echoed echoed echoed

and trying to drown the lies out
clamorous din
exposed the truth
as it looped and weaved
through all of those
who thought they were honest

## Mind Numbing

the lone voice of solitude
howls
the introvert mind
overwhelmed by waves
cluttered
reading thoughts
unable to think

our telepaphone
never a busy signal
free long distance too

#

thinking juicy thoughts
inappropriate unless
you're at the juice bar

our minds unified
seek quietude once again
at peace without words

#

a solitary
broadcast joins the multitude
crying in the rain

**The Answering Machine**

our brains were connected with a wire
quaint, reminiscent of a landline
no one was impressed
short distance telepathy
easily out strode
satellites circled overhead
ever connecting

still, our communication was direct
instantaneous
all this work, this miracle
could have been spoken out loud
to the same effect
so, telepathy went the way
of the answering machine
spending the rest of its days
in a museum of dated tech

moving from the future
directly to the past
we leapfrogged like a flip phone

## The Mind

when the mind was a mystery
when the mind was a machine
when the mind was a clock
when the mind was a radio
when the mind was a TV
when the mind was a computer
when will the mind be the mind

**The Volume**

it's so loud in here
privacy barely a memory
crosstalk into babble
trying to remember when
thoughts were my own
again interrupted
by the masses
proximity become curse

the dreams are the worst
chaotic floods
emotions without context
all thoughts at once
strangers, so many strangers
and it's so loud in here

**Pictureless**

images forced their way in
my aphant mind
strobing without reference
searching for reference
with no mind's eye
hideous synesthesia

and when you looked
the feelings came
all blank black and heavy
sonorous, aromatic, tactile
my pictureless harsh
came upon you
without reference

**Brains**

all those little brains
moving in unison
flock never collides
school survives the gnash
hivemind communism
never a word

all those big brains
full of abstraction and stars
trying to know everything
birthing the word
thoughts cloud
mouthing the word "alone"

# Odes to Women of Science

**Ada Lovelace**

buried with the misguided genius
seeing through nature, you did more than compensate
with symbol – all the way past mathematics
into abstractions of boundless expression

giving mind to the engine
harmony out of the cold
unwelcome for prejudice
nonetheless transcending

thanks to Turing's reminder
we can run the punch cards of your thoughts
and you touch us with your grand insight
daily, in all things
even your dream of flight

at least one of your bets paid off
as the loom weaves
nature back into numbers

**Mae C. Jemison**

dancer in space
model for self-actualization
never losing purpose
giving meaning to Endeavor

whether in the camps or Enterprise
symbol of determination
remind us, "there is always hope"
leap from the floor to the heavens

your dream comes true for us all
as if zero G
is there for movement
of the first dancer in space

**Lene Vestergaard Hau**

harnessing the incomprehensible
changing the speed limit
thought into condensate
information will not be lost

through your slow glass
your frozen clouds
the photon speaks
at human speeds

are you the time traveler
of the small distances
has the cosmos changed
as pulses filter from nature

when you turn it back into light
may your name be solidified
in the permanent waves

**Rosalind Franklin**

as they scoffed at you during lunch
you saw the geometry of the small
wielding the x-ray
like a giant eye

if you knew of the theft
you moved on, faith, you said
equaled the improvement of humankind
still, you deserve the prize

you are proof that being silenced
cannot stop one woman
from bettering our knowledge
or deepening our understanding
of who we are

**Valentina Tereshkova**

the day the sky took off its hat
you gave every woman the cosmos
not quite the train you imagined
as a girl, proof of dreams real

from farm to factory to mill
to space, you landed again in the fields
shared milk and gave space to the people
Mother Russia incarnate

still humble, "as war children we dreamt of peace"
even though they almost lost you to the heavens
you point to Mars
the Seagull cannot be grounded for long

## Eleanor 'Glo' Helin

scan the plates for those near us
the small, unglamorous bodies
counting the countless stones
moving baby picture specks

there may come a time
when your efforts save us all
flung from orbit
death trajectory

floating mountains of stone
ice, metal – gavel of the skies
you see them coming

the planet that wasn't
debris field of discovery
honored with your name

# Miscellaneous Poems

**Augmented**

all sensors replaced
    I see you from a mile away
    touch with polymers
    smell from a distance
all organs augmented
    EM field perceived
    widened spectrum
    time moving slowly
all eyes stare
    cannot see as I do
    judge when seeing
    seeing only change
all misunderstand
    magnetic fields tell me
    stress levels deeper than scent
    no one can relate
all nine senses
    become animal
    or something more
    they do not see me as human

**Chipped**

they put a chip in my brain
said it would speed up thoughts
clearly weren't thinking about sleep
but now I am, lots, and fast

hunger, heartrate, digestion
chip rode those too
hair's gone gray
and I'm thinking about it all

so quickly I decide
it was a bad idea
computing what's next
I think about Dea…

**Private Beauty**

the chips made us a hive
every intention known
an enormous flash of surprises
     they were the last
we moved in unison
like the films of soldiers
without war, they were/are us
we looped into one set of thoughts
individuality gone, problems solved
things of the past: disagreement, conflict
art, poetry – they died too
so I seek the scalpel
cut this chip out
hoping for the chaotic private beauty

**Snitched**

mech tech hectic
firewall privacy down
hivemind thought flood
dug at the implant for hours
electronic pimple
succeeded in breaking skin
not contact, still thick
bloodied fingers, red handed
they storm the door
long since onto me
the collective rat
giving it all away
in real time

**Woof**

the decommissioned robodogs
     advertised as companions for the elderly
would get you off the hook
     for caring for loved ones
               …loved…
     blowup doll intimacy
it didn't matter that they were a disaster
     on the battlefield
     now they were domesticated
for a hefty price
     they could care for your parents
     lying limbless from the same
               …disastrous war…
give them chipper names like Rex
     you can hardly tell the difference
     turrets replaced by grinning screens
and they will be oh-so-familiar
     entering the battlefield of old age
shining reminders of everything that went wrong

**Equalizer**

the great inevitable
feared by so many, if not all
common as a sunny day
as obvious as snow
the great motivator
battling against entropy
knowing there is no victor
still ices hearts
in anticipation
close brushes bring the laughter
of relief
and the other guy is always better
the great mount
for which there is no peak
the trough
for which all peaks must bow
though it is not something down
below has no real significance
the ground which calls us all
has no menace
or meaning
soil, that great death, equalizer
rich as shit
is heaven so far from your permanent birthday

**Imbibing with the Spirits**

imbibing with the spirits
fluidic passage through the flesh
they animate devilishly
contacting matter
heeding every temptation
unavailable on the other side of the veil

tongue becomes whip
fist into hammer
heart into desire

Legion comes forth
sees through glassy eyes, the multitude
moves on the plane
denied them for most of eternity

mind into chorus
imbibing with the spirits

**Sighting**

classic saucer
though bright red
hovering still
in mountain air
multiple tiers
antennae tail
does not move
or leave a trail
some that see
still don't believe
others saw bodies retrieved
I know what I saw
in that spring sky
binoculars, not naked eye
everyone saw what they wanted to
convinced ourselves of what was true

**Sun-Like**

couple of times
in reach
this is it
kindling it was

house burned
dog dead
ashes to make clay

those stars never stopped
seemed like Hell, lots
the long times
all the black in-between

that old shovel dings against a rock sometimes
rattles the wrist in a bad way
in reach, so to say
building up a new house
all tinder ripe for fire
burning in the good way
all sun-like
and eternal for now

**To Possess**

possessing a body isn't all it's cracked up to be
on one side they crawl all over each other
to get in the fresh ones
on the other side, we trick our way in
looked down on for it, too
*it's unnatural* – blah, blah, blah

once you're in
it's all gravity
painfully slow getting round
and the aches and pains
maybe that's why they claw at the freshies

when *we* got in
it was all a mess
what a clunker
all that work
just to learn
that it was already torturing itself

**The Price**

reaching the summit
of the mountain of skulls
caving under its own weight
underfoot, balance loosens
foundations of evil
unstable as the minds of the killers
who climb in search
of the heaven they are destroying
thinking it their possession
as if every skull
didn't contain a mind
equal in life
and in death
they march to doom's thunderous drums
self-righteous in their folly
exacting a price
which they must borrow to pay
their debt to humanity
soon to be extracted
in Hell

## The Picture

presumably it was mothers
holding up pictures of their young
sounded like mourning
we'd seen it before
over and over
whittled down to media trope

there's lots of reasons
for someone to hold up a picture of a face
pain sounds like pain though
my Ma would shriek
we recognized nothing about them
except pain sounds like pain

**Exoarbor**

glacier, coral, tree
the real book of time
counting our spirals
this system's record
ticking off seasons
unique to our place
relative vantage

in another system
habitable zone far from star
axis degrees differ
still branching universal
one to two, two to four
relative rings

compare these cores
orbits – so many circles
life is counting

**Post**

as it died
face indistinguishable
unreadable to me, anyway
it sang
tones nearly as vague
meaning, intent, design
lost on this foreigner

the song never went away
nightly blank face opens to repeat
trying to sing along
physiology won't allow
nothing but memory
no way to share

a childhood song
the names of its offspring
a dying curse to ensnare their killer
never to know
never did we speak
as the violence roiled on

## POV

the so-called sodomy laws
    fell apart in my cloaca
drones flew to the window
    POV'd through private scenes
        made quadruple X films
            as they removed my skins
one of a kind, they decided
    to legislate our love
        even after all the tests
            killing dignity and function
on my world normalcy blurs
    their alien sense of morality
        they came upon me
            all knives in their hearts
their poison duality, so singular
    in their understanding
        of real oneness
            thinks my being
has something to do with them
    or their business

**Ego Death**

once I found your speed
tunneling toward Death
ego smeared in the spiral
laughter in the shape of tears

at this speed time stills
reference irrelevant
"I" dies, replaced
something grander, encompassing
we cannot measure the stillness
which moves from our position
both at once
outside our frameworks

will I know your speed again
more than ego will die
whence I return
may we join

## The Big Pop

universe
multiverse
universe
multiverse
Einstein-Rosen bridge
multiverse
multiverse

**The Big Dreams**

those flying cars we dreamed of…
	on the way…*ish*
pills for food
	not such a great idea, really
jumpsuits
	ever had to pee with one on, a pain

our dreams were kinda small
	skipped right over the big stuff
Equality for all
enough food for all
clean water… clean sky…
	we let "progress" trample those

let the big dreams come
dream them together
bring those dreams right out of heaven
and down to the ground

# Acknowledgements

Utopian Problems, Time's Arrow, & The Telepathy Machine first appeared as mini-chapbooks from Space Cowboy Books. Musical audiobook versions of these chapbooks can be downloaded for free at

https://spacecowboybooks.bandcamp.com/

Odes to Women of Science first appeared in Cholla Needles Magazine

Chipped, Private Beauty, & Augmented first appeared in Dark Matter Magazine

Sun-Like, The Big Pop, Ego Death, & Equalizer first appeared in Eccentric Orbits

Woof first appeared in Star*Line

Snitched first appeared in Eye to the Telescope

Imbibing with the Spirits, To Possess & The Price first appeared in the SFPA Halloween Page

Sighting first appeared in The Flying Saucer Poetry Review

The Big Dreams first appeared in Dreadnought SF

# About the Author

Jean-Paul L. Garnier is the owner of Space Cowboy Books bookstore and publishing house, producer of *Simultaneous Times* Podcast (2023 & 25 Laureate Award Winner, 2024 BSFA, Ignyte, and British Fantasy Award Finalist), and was the editor of the SFPA's *Star*Line* magazine from 2021-2025. He is currently the poetry editor of *Worlds of IF & Galaxy* magazines. In 2024 he won the Laureate Award for Best Editor. He has written many books of poetry and science fiction.

https://spacecowboybooks.com/

**More Books by the Author**

Poetry:

*The Future is Brief*

*Proving Grounds*

*Betelgeuse Dimming*

*Future Anthropology*


Fiction:

*Cardboard Spaceship*

*Black Line Trail*

*In Each Other's Arms*

*Garbage In, Gospel Out*

*Echo of Creation*

SPACE
COWBOY

9 781968 958022